Listen,
My Children

POEMS FOR FIRST GRADERS

A CORE KNOWLEDGE® BOOK

LISTEN MY CHILDREN: POEMS FOR FIRST GRADERS
ONE IN A SERIES, *POEMS FOR KINDERGARTNERS—FIFTH GRADERS*,
COLLECTING THE POEMS IN THE *CORE KNOWLEDGE SEQUENCE*

A CORE KNOWLEDGE® BOOK

SERIES EDITOR: SUSAN TYLER HITCHCOCK
RESEARCHER: JEANNE NICHOLSON SILER
POETRY CONSULTANT: STEPHEN B. CUSHMAN
GENERAL EDITOR: E. D. HIRSCH, JR.

LIBRARY OF CONGRESS CARD CATALOG NUMBER: 00-111615
FIFTEENTH PRINTING; MAY 2017
ISBN: 978-1890517-29-8

PRINTED IN CANADA
DESIGN BY DIANE NELSON GRAPHIC DESIGN
COVER ILLUSTRATION BY LANCE HIDY, LANCE@LANCEHIDY.COM

CORE KNOWLEDGE FOUNDATION
801 EAST HIGH STREET
CHARLOTTESVILLE, VIRGINIA 22902
WWW.COREKNOWLEDGE.ORG

About this Book

"LISTEN, MY CHILDREN, and you shall hear . . ." So begins a famous poem about Paul Revere, written by Henry Wadsworth Longfellow in 1855. This opening line reminds us that every time we read a poem, we hear that poem as well. The sounds and rhythms of the words are part of the poem's meaning. Poems are best understood when read out loud, or when a reader hears the sounds of the words in his or her head while reading silently.

This six-volume series collects many of the poems in the *Core Knowledge Sequence* for kindergarten through fifth grade. Each volume includes occasional notes about the poems and biographical sketches about the poems' authors, but the focus is really the poems themselves. Some have been chosen because they reflect times past; others because of their literary fame; still others were selected because they express states of mind shared by many children.

This selection of poetry, part of the *Core Knowledge Sequence*, is based on the work of E. D. Hirsch, Jr., author of *Cultural Literacy* and *The Schools We Need*. The *Sequence* outlines a core curriculum for preschool through grade eight in English and language arts, history and geography, math, science, the fine arts, and music. It is designed to ensure that children are exposed to the essential knowledge that establishes cultural literacy as they also acquire a broad, firm foundation for higher-level schooling. Its first version was developed in 1990 at a convention of teachers and subject matter experts. Revised in 1995 to reflect the classroom experience of Core Knowledge teachers, the *Sequence* is now used in hundreds of schools across America. Its content also guides the Core Knowledge Series, *What Your Kindergartner–Sixth Grader Needs to Know*.

Contents

Sing a Song of People   6
Lois Lenski

Rope Rhyme   8
Eloise Greenfield

Solomon Grundy   9
Author unknown

The Purple Cow   9
Gelett Burgess

The Swing   11
Robert Louis Stevenson

Table Manners   12
Gelett Burgess

I Know All the Sounds that the Animals Make   13
Jack Prelutsky

The Owl and the Pussycat   14
Edward Lear

Wynken, Blynken, and Nod   16
Eugene Field

Thanksgiving Day   19
Lydia Maria Child

Washington   21
Nancy Byrd Turner

My Shadow   22
Robert Louis Stevenson

Hope   25
Langston Hughes

The Pasture   27
Robert Frost

———— FOR ADDITIONAL READING ————

The Caterpillar   28
Christina Rossetti

Written in March   29
William Wordsworth

The Land of Story-Books   30
Robert Louis Stevenson

Acknowledgments   32

Sing a Song of People
by Lois Lenski

Sing a song of people
   Walking fast or slow;
People in the city,
   Up and down they go.

People on the sidewalk,
People on the bus;
People passing, passing,
In back and front of us.
People on the subway
Underneath the ground;
People riding taxis
Round and round and round.

People with their hats on,
Going in the doors;
People with umbrellas
When it rains and pours.
People in tall buildings
And in stores below;
Riding elevators
Up and down they go.

People walking singly,
People in a crowd;
People saying nothing,
People talking loud.
People laughing, smiling,
Grumpy people too;
People who just hurry
And never look at you!

Sing a song of people
    Who like to come and go;
Sing a song of city people
    You see but never know!

Rope Rhyme

by Eloise Greenfield

Get set, ready now, jump right in
Bounce and kick and giggle and spin
Listen to the rope when it hits the ground
Listen to that clappedy-slappedy sound
Jump right up when it tells you to
Come back down, whatever you do
Count to a hundred, count by ten
Start to count all over again
That's what jumping is all about
Get set, ready now,
                    jump
                         right
                              out!

Solomon Grundy
Author unknown

Solomon Grundy
Born on a Monday,
Christened on Tuesday,
Married on Wednesday,
Took ill on Thursday,
Worse on Friday,
Died on Saturday,
Buried on Sunday.
This is the end of
Solomon Grundy.

The Purple Cow
by Gelett Burgess

I never saw a Purple Cow,
  I never hope to see one;
But I can tell you, anyhow,
  I'd rather see than be one!

Robert Louis Stevenson
1850–1894

Robert Louis Stevenson, an English author, wrote in many different styles. He wrote sweet, happy poems for children in *A Child's Garden of Verses.* He wrote exciting adventures, such as the novel *Treasure Island.* He also wrote a horror story called *Dr. Jekyll and Mr. Hyde.*

The Swing

by Robert Louis Stevenson

How do you like to go up in a swing,
　　Up in the air so blue?
Oh, I do think it the pleasantest thing
　　Ever a child can do!

Up in the air and over the wall,
　　Till I can see so wide,
Rivers and trees and cattle and all
　　Over the countryside—

Till I look down on the garden green,
　　Down on the roof so brown—
Up in the air I go flying again,
　　Up in the air and down!

Table Manners

by Gelett Burgess

The Goops they lick their fingers,
    And the Goops they lick their knives;
They spill their broth on the tablecloth—
    Oh, they lead disgusting lives!
The Goops they talk while eating,
    And loud and fast they chew;
And that is why I'm glad that I
    Am not a Goop—are you?

I Know All the Sounds
That the Animals Make

by Jack Prelutsky

I know all the sounds that the animals make,
and make them all day from the moment I wake,
I roar like a mouse and I purr like a moose,
I hoot like a duck and I moo like a goose.

I squeak like a cat and I quack like a frog,
I oink like a bear and I honk like a hog,
I croak like a cow and I bark like a bee,
no wonder the animals marvel at me.

The Owl and the Pussycat

by Edward Lear

The Owl and the Pussycat went to sea
    In a beautiful pea-green boat,
They took some honey, and plenty of money,
    Wrapped up in a five-pound note.
The Owl looked up to the stars above,
    And sang to a small guitar,
"O lovely Pussy! O Pussy, my love,
    What a beautiful Pussy you are,
        You are,
        You are!
What a beautiful Pussy you are!"

Pussy said to the Owl, "You elegant fowl!
    How charmingly sweet you sing!

FIVE-POUND NOTE The English version of a five-dollar bill.

O let us be married! Too long we have tarried:
　　But what shall we do for a ring?"
They sailed away for a year and a day,
　　To the land where the Bong-tree grows
And there in a wood a Piggy-wig stood
　　With a ring at the end of his nose,
　　　　His nose,
　　　　His nose,
　　With a ring at the end of his nose.

"Dear Pig, are you willing to sell for one shilling
　　Your ring?" Said the Piggy, "I will."
So they took it away, and were married next day
　　By the Turkey who lives on the hill.
They dined on the mince, and slices of quince,
　　Which they ate with a runcible spoon;
And hand in hand, on the edge of the sand,
　　They danced by the light of the moon,
　　　　The moon,
　　　　The moon,
They danced by the light of the moon.

SHILLING
An English coin, not worth a lot.

MINCE
Chopped spiced fruit, often made into mincemeat pie.

QUINCE
A fruit like an apple that grows on bushes.

Edward Lear made up the term "runcible" spoon. Since then, though, people have come to use the word for something real: an eating utensil curved like a spoon but pronged like a fork.

Wynken, Blynken, and Nod

by Eugene Field

Wynken, Blynken, and Nod one night
    Sailed off in a wooden shoe—
Sailed on a river of crystal light
    Into a sea of dew.
"Where are you going, and what do you wish?"
    The old moon asked the three.
"We have come to fish for the herring fish
    That live in this beautiful sea;
    Nets of silver and gold have we,"
            Said Wynken,
            Blynken,
            And Nod.

The old moon laughed and sang a song,
    As they rocked in the wooden shoe;
And the wind that sped them all night long
    Ruffled the waves of dew.
The little stars were the herring fish
    That lived in that beautiful sea;
"Now cast your nets wherever you wish,
    Never afeared are we!"
    So cried the stars to the fishermen three,
            Wynken,
            Blynken,
            And Nod.

All night long their nets they threw
    To the stars in the twinkling foam;
Then down from the skies came the wooden shoe,
    Bringing the fishermen home.
'Twas all so pretty a sail, it seemed
    As if it could not be;
And some folk thought 'twas a dream they'd dreamed
    Of sailing that beautiful sea;
    But I shall name you the fishermen three:
            Wynken,
            Blynken,
            And Nod.

Wynken and Blynken are two little eyes,
    And Nod is a little head,
And the wooden shoe that sailed the skies
    Is a wee one's trundle-bed;
So shut your eyes while Mother sings
    Of wonderful sights that be,
And you shall see the beautiful things
    As you rock in the misty sea
    Where the old shoe rocked the fishermen three,
                Wynken,
                Blynken,
                And Nod.

TRUNDLE-BED
A low bed with wheels that can be rolled underneath a taller bed.

Thanksgiving Day
by Lydia Maria Child

Over the river and through the wood,
    To grandfather's house we go;
        The horse knows the way
        To carry the sleigh
    Through the white and drifted snow.

Over the river and through the wood—
    Oh, how the wind does blow!
        It stings the toes
        And bites the nose,
    As over the ground we go.

Over the river and through the wood,
    To have a first-rate play.
        Hear the bells ring,
        "Ting-a-ling-ding!"
    Hurrah for Thanksgiving Day!

Over the river and through the wood,

    Trot fast, my dapple-gray!

        Spring over the ground,

        Like a hunting-hound!

    For this is Thanksgiving Day.

DAPPLE-GRAY
The color of a horse: light grey with white spots.

Over the river and through the wood—

    And straight through the barn-yard gate.

        We seem to go

        Extremely slow—

    It is so hard to wait!

Over the river and through the wood—

    Now Grandmother's cap I spy!

        Hurrah for the fun!

        Is the pudding done?

    Hurrah for the pumpkin-pie!

Washington

by Nancy Byrd Turner

He played by the river when he was young,
He raced with rabbits along the hills,
He fished for minnows, and climbed and swung,
And hooted back at the whippoorwills.
Strong and slender and tall he grew—
And then, one morning, the bugles blew.

WHIPPOORWILL
A bird with a distinctive call that sounds like its name.

Over the hills the summons came,
Over the river's shining rim.
He said that the bugles called his name,
He knew that his country needed him,
And he answered, "Coming!" and marched away
For many a night and many a day.

Perhaps when the marches were hot and long
He'd think of the river flowing by
Or, camping under the winter sky,
Would hear the whippoorwill's far-off song.
Boy or soldier, in peace or strife,
He loved America all his life!

My Shadow

by Robert Louis Stevenson

I have a little shadow that goes in and out with me,

And what can be the use of him is more than I can see.

He is very, very like me from the heels up to the head;

And I see him jump before me, when I jump into my bed.

INDIA-RUBBER BALL
A rubber ball from the time when most rubber came from the country of India.

The funniest thing about him is the way he likes to grow—
Not at all like proper children, which is always very slow;
For he sometimes shoots up taller like an India-rubber ball,
And he sometimes gets so little that there's none of
    him at all.

He hasn't got a notion of how children ought to play,
And can only make a fool of me in every sort of way.
He stays so close beside me, he's a coward you can see;
I'd think shame to stick to nursie as that shadow
    sticks to me!

One morning, very early, before the sun was up,
I rose and found the shining dew on every buttercup;
But my lazy little shadow, like an arrant sleepy-head,
Had stayed at home behind me and was fast asleep
    in bed.

Langston Hughes
1902–1967

Langston Hughes was an important writer during the
"Harlem Renaissance," when many African-American
artists and performers worked together in New York
and made wonderful works of art. Altogether Langston
Hughes wrote sixteen books of poetry, twenty plays,
two novels, and lots of stories.

Hope

by Langston Hughes

Sometimes when I'm lonely,
Don't know why,
Keep thinkin' I won't be lonely
By and by.

Robert Frost
1874–1963

Robert Frost was one of America's best-known and best-loved poets in the 20th century. He lived much of the time on a farm in New Hampshire, and many of his poems describe life in the country.

The Pasture

by Robert Frost

I'm going out to clean the pasture spring;
I'll only stop to rake the leaves away
(And wait to watch the water clear, I may):
I shan't be gone long.—You come too.

I'm going out to fetch the little calf
That's standing by the mother. It's so young
It totters when she licks it with her tongue.
I shan't be gone long.—You come too.

The Caterpillar

by Christina Rossetti

Brown and furry
Caterpillar in a hurry
Take your walk
To the shady leaf or stalk
Or what not,
Which may be your chosen spot.
No toad spy you,
Hovering birds of prey pass by you;
Spin and die,
To live again a butterfly.

Written in March
by William Wordsworth

The cock is crowing,
The stream is flowing,
The small birds twitter,
The lake doth glitter,
The green field sleeps in the sun;
The oldest and youngest
Are at work with the strongest;
The cattle are grazing,
Their heads never raising;
There are forty feeding like one!

Like an army defeated
The snow hath retreated,
And now doth fare ill
On the top of the bare hill;
The ploughboy is whooping—anon—anon:
There's joy in the mountains;
There's life in the fountains;
Small clouds are sailing,
Blue sky prevailing;
The rain is over and gone!

DOTH FARE ILL
Does not do well.

PLOUGHBOY
A young man who works in the fields with a plough.

PREVAILING
Taking over.

The Land of Story-Books
by Robert Louis Stevenson

At evening when the lamp is lit,
Around the fire my parents sit;
They sit at home and talk and sing,
And do not play at anything.

Now, with my little gun I crawl
All in the dark along the wall,
And follow round the forest track
Away behind the sofa back.

There, in the night, where none can spy,
All in my hunter's camp I lie,
And play at books that I have read
Till it is time to go to bed.

These are the hills, these are the woods,
These are my starry solitudes;
And there the river by whose brink
The roaring lions come to drink.

I see the others far away
As if in firelit camp they lay,
And I, like to an Indian scout,
Around their party prowled about.

So, when my nurse comes in for me,
Home I return across the sea,
And go to bed with backward looks
At my dear land of Story-Books.

Acknowledgments

Every care has been taken to trace and acknowledge copyright of the poems and images in this volume. If accidental infringement has occurred, the editor offers apologies and welcomes communications that allow proper acknowledgment in subsequent editions.

"Sing a Song of People" from *The Life I Live* by Lois Lenski. Copyright © 1956. Reprinted by permission of SLL/Sterling Lord Literistic, Inc.

"Rope Rhyme" from *Honey, I Love and Other Love Poems*, by Eloise Greenfield. Copyright © 1978 by Eloise Greenfield. Used by permission of HarperCollins Publishers.

"Hope" from *The Collected Poems of Langston Hughes* by Langston Hughes, edited by Arnold Rampersad with David Roessel, Associate Editor. Copyright © 1994 by the Estate of Langston Hughes. Used by permission of Alfred A. Knopf, an imprint of Random House, LLC. All rights reserved.

"I Know All the Sounds that the Animals Make" from *Something Big Has Been Here* by Jack Prelutsky. Copyright © 1990 by Jack Prelutsky. Used by permission of HarperCollins Publishing.

Images:
Robert Louis Stevenson: © Bettmann/CORBIS
Langston Hughes: © CORBIS
Robert Frost: © Hulton-Deutsch Collection/CORBIS

Illustrations by G. B. McIntosh, pages 16, 22, 25.